Rachel Carson
Nature's Guardian

Gina Dal Fuoco

Earth and Space Science Readers:
Rachel Carson:
Nature's Guardian

Publishing Credits

Editorial Director
Dona Herweck Rice

Creative Director
Lee Aucoin

Associate Editor
Joshua BishopRoby

Illustration Manager
Timothy J. Bradley

Editor-in-Chief
Sharon Coan, M.S.Ed.

Publisher
Rachelle Cracchiolo, M.S.Ed.

Science Contributor
Sally Ride Science

Science Consultants
Nancy McKeown,
    Planetary Geologist
William B. Rice,
    Engineering Geologist

Teacher Created Materials

5301 Oceanus Drive
Huntington Beach, CA 92649-1030
http://www.tcmpub.com
ISBN 978-0-7439-0566-4

Table of Contents

The Girl by the River

In a farmhouse near a river, there lived a little girl. She was born on May 27, 1907, the third child of Robert and Maria Carson. She grew up in the small town of Springdale, Pennsylvania. Her name was Rachel Carson.

The little girl and her mother loved to spend time together. They explored the forest and streams. They watched flowers grow and birds fly. Sometimes they just sat

Rachel Carson ➡

The Allegheny River flows near where Carson grew up.

and looked at the beautiful world around them. This is where Rachel Carson's love of nature began.

She also loved to write. She published her first magazine article when she was only ten years old. She won an award for her story called "A Battle in the Clouds." When she grew up, she went to college to become a writer.

▼ Carson loved the sea as much as the land.

Writing for Children

When she was grown up, Carson wrote a book for children. It was called *A Sense of Wonder.* She wanted to encourage parents to take their children into nature.

Rachel Said

"I can remember no time, even in earliest childhood, when I didn't assume I was going to be a writer. Also, I can remember no time when I wasn't interested in the out-of-doors and the whole world of nature. Those interests, I know, I inherited from my mother and have always shared with her."

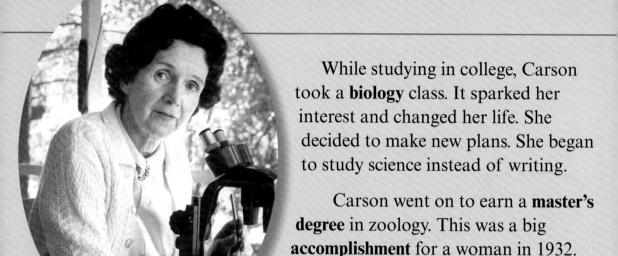
Rachel Carson

While studying in college, Carson took a **biology** class. It sparked her interest and changed her life. She decided to make new plans. She began to study science instead of writing.

Carson went on to earn a **master's degree** in zoology. This was a big **accomplishment** for a woman in 1932. Not many women then went to college. Those who did often studied things to help them be better homemakers. It was rare for a woman to become a scientist, but that's exactly what Carson did.

She also became the first woman ever to pass the **civil service** test. This test lets a person work for the U.S. government. She decided to work for the U.S. Bureau of Fisheries. She worked as a biologist and writer. So, she was able to do the two things she loved.

During this time, Carson wrote about Earth's **natural resources**. She wanted to help people better understand nature. She knew that Earth's resources are finite. If we use them up too quickly or in unhealthy ways, we will damage the earth. And we may not have what we need for survival. Carson wanted others to help care for the planet. She wanted to teach people that they are only one part of nature and not the rulers of it.

Family Life

After Carson's father died in 1935, she lived with and supported her mother. When Carson's sister died two years later, Carson raised her two nieces. She also adopted and raised her niece's son after her niece died. Carson never married.

Carson became interested in the ocean while in college. She spent one summer working at a marine lab. After college, she had a short radio program. It was called "Romance Under the Waters." She taught about the strange world of the ocean.

Carson wrote three books about ocean life. People liked her books. She wrote about difficult science facts, but she made them interesting. Even someone who wasn't a scientist could understand what she was writing about. It was important to her that people understand the underwater world.

While working for the government, Carson became worried about the oceans. She studied the use of **chemical pesticides**. They are chemicals used to kill bugs and insects. But if pesticides can kill pests, couldn't they also hurt other living things? Carson suspected that pesticides harmed ocean animals. She knew she had to warn the public. They had to know about the dangers of pesticides.

This farmer is spraying pesticides on his crop of flowers.

Rainwater runoff picks up pesticides on land and leaves them in the ocean.

A Way with Words

Rachel Carson's second book was her most popular of the time. It is called *The Sea Around Us*. It was published in 32 languages!

Top 100

TIME Magazine included Rachel Carson in its list of the 100 most influential people of the 20th Century.

Fish and Wildlife

The United States Fish and Wildlife Service was created in 1940. The service was started to protect the **environment** for both people and wildlife. It first studied why the fish population was declining. The goal was to solve the problem.

Rachel Carson was hired as one of the first female scientists there. She worked with others to study the effects of **DDT**. DDT is a type of pesticide. During this time, it was widely used to destroy pests. People didn't realize it was doing a lot of other damage, too.

Sea lions bask on the rocks of Monterey Bay.

Important Work

The U.S. Fish and Wildlife Service has more than 40,000 volunteers. They do over one million hours of work each year! Today, the Fish and Wildlife Service still tries to solve problems in the environment around the world.

Marine Biology

Many people think that marine biologists spend their days out at sea or playing with dolphins. That's only part of what they do. Only a very small number of people get to work directly with these animals.

Some marine biologists work with animals at zoos and aquariums. These places used to keep animals just for people to look at. Today, they are becoming more and more important in protecting animal life. They help teach people about animal issues. They also help animals that are in danger.

Working with animals isn't easy. Getting a good education about animals may be the best thing you can do to help them.

Marine scientists in the field tag a loggerhead turtle.

Pests and Pesticides

A pest is a living thing that is someplace it isn't wanted or is doing damage. It might be an animal such as a mouse or bug. It might be an unwanted plant.

Pesticides are chemicals that kill pests or their young. Farmers have been helped by the use of pesticides. They can grow more crops with less waste. But what's the cost to our environment?

Pesticides kill pests. They can harm other things, too. They stay in the soil for many years. Pesticides can have serious effects on people, too. They get into the crops that people eat. They seep into the water in the ground that people drink.

◄ international symbol for biohazards and poisons

⬆ Pesticides would be sprayed on fields from airplanes called crop dusters.

Did you know?

More than 500 insect pests and 270 weeds are now **resistant** to one or more pesticides. Over time, they have learned to live with the pesticide. The pesticide no longer destroys them.

Wangari Maathai

Who is Wangari Maathai? Like Rachel Carson, she is an environmentalist. Maathai was born in Kenya. She went to college in America and earned two degrees. Then Maathai earned her Ph.D. in Kenya. Some didn't think she could do it. She proved them wrong!

In 1986, Maathai started the Green Belt movement. She was worried too many trees were being cut down. People weren't planting new trees. For every 100 trees cut, only nine were being planted. **Deforestation** was causing many problems. Lack of trees meant lack of food and shelter for animals. It meant lack of firewood for people. Even water became polluted without the natural balance of tree life.

With Maathai's help, women in Kenyan villages plant trees. In this way, they are helping the environment. They also earn money for their work. They can better care for their children and their futures. In 2004, Maathai won the Nobel Peace Prize for her work.

DDT

Farmers used to have a hard time dealing with insects and weeds that damaged their crops. They needed something to help them.

A scientist named Paul Muller developed the chemical known as DDT as a pesticide. At first, it seemed great for farming. It killed the pests. It was strong and long lasting. However, this is what made it so toxic to the environment. It stayed in soil and water. It stayed in plant and animal tissue. This made it dangerous for many years after it was used.

DDT is no longer used in the United States because of its serious harm to animals and people. For example, pelicans became an endangered species because of DDT. It caused their egg shells to become fragile and break easily. With no new babies, a species will die out.

Still Around

DDT has not been used in the United States since 1972. But a scientist recently found high levels of the pesticide in songbirds that live in the United States.

Wheat is sprayed with DDT.

Insect pests eat the DDT. Most die, but not right away.

Birds eat the insects and are poisoned by the DDT.

14

Rosalie Barrow Edge

Rosalie Barrow was born into a wealthy family in New York City in 1877. She grew up and married. She went to many fancy parties, but she wanted to make a difference in the world. In 1913, she met an interesting woman named Lady Rhondda who would change her life. The woman was active in fighting for women's rights. Edge jumped right into action to join the fight. She wanted to help when something was wrong.

Later, she became interested in birds. She started to fight for birds just as she had for women. For example, she uncovered some of the things the Audubon Society was doing. The Audubon Society was started to study and protect wildlife. But hunting was allowed in some areas the society was supposed to be protecting. Edge exposed this. Then, during the 1930s, she created a wildlife sanctuary called the Hawk Mountain Sanctuary. People still visit there. They can see hawks, falcons, and eagles. It has educational and research programs to make a lasting difference.

Silent Spring

Silent Spring was Rachel Carson's most important book. It is also considered by some to be the most influential book of the past 50 years. She started writing it in 1958, and it was published in 1962. It discussed the effects of DDT and other pesticides. Carson taught people to look at the natural world in a new way.

The title of Carson's book has to do with the normal noises of springtime. New life comes to be in the spring. Bees buzz, birds chirp, frogs ribbit, and the world comes alive. But what would the world be like if the spring were silent? What if we did so much damage to the planet that the new life never came?

◄ Carson at the time *Silent Spring* was published

Carson's book made many people very upset. Some people were making a lot of money selling the chemicals. Farmers were angry about her book. They needed chemicals to grow bigger crops. People were so angry that they said and wrote terrible things about her.

Despite the attacks, *Silent Spring* made the government look into the use of DDT. Carson got people to see the dangerous effects of pesticides. They were hurting the planet and humans. This was the beginning of the modern environmental movement. People used to see the natural world and the human world as separate things. Carson's book made people see the connection between the two. If humans harmed the natural world, then they were also harming the human world.

Look Who's Reading

President John F. Kennedy read Carson's book. He had Congress investigate the use and effects of DDT. This is why DDT was banned in the United States. Many people believe that Carson's book is also a big reason why the Environmental Protection Agency was started.

Gone Too Soon

Sadly, Rachel Carson died in 1964 after a long battle with cancer.

When *Silent Spring* was written, Europe had already banned the use of mercury oxide to cover seeds. It took Carson's book to get the United States to do the same.

⬆ The ocean is a very large and delicate world.

Changing Our Ideas About Nature

Nature is always changing. Some events might not seem important. Scientists discover why some events really are important. Things like pollution have many effects that can't always be easily seen. The first signs of damage often show up in ocean life. Scientists study ocean life so they can understand what may happen to our entire planet.

Carson wanted people to understand our relationship with nature. Humans are just one link in the chain. When we damage one of the links, we weaken our own. For example, we are all part of a **food web.** Each piece of the food web is closely tied to the others. When something happens to one piece of the web, there is an effect on the others. This helps to keep the balance of plant and animal populations. We see this in the example of seals, squid, and sharks. When there are too many seals in one place, there will not be enough squid for them to eat. Many of the seals will starve and die. Fewer seals mean less food for the sharks. Some sharks will starve to death. When there are fewer sharks, the seal population will rise again.

People are also part of a food web. Our actions affect our food sources. Earth depends on the harmony of all these food webs.

That is exactly the kind of thing that Carson was talking about. We are all connected. What one species does affects all the other species. Humans are the most intelligent species on the planet. It is the job of every human to protect and preserve the planet for every living thing.

a simple energy pyramid

Ecosystem

An **ecosystem** is a community of living things in an environment and the environment itself, all working together. Carson introduced the word "ecosystem" in *Silent Spring*.

▲ John Muir

Other people have also believed in the importance of the environment. One of them was John Muir. He had a lot in common with Rachel Carson. His love for nature started when he was just a boy. He was a writer, too. He wrote to share his love of nature with the world. Muir also shared the value of taking care of nature.

Muir was a **preservationist**. That is someone who works to preserve, or keep and protect, the environment or something else of worth. He started the Sierra Club. Its goal was to save California's Sierra Mountains. Muir thought the mountain areas should be available to the public. He took groups to the Sierras to enjoy their beauty.

▼ Before John Muir and the Sierra Club, taking a trip into the Sierra Mountains took a lot of preparation!

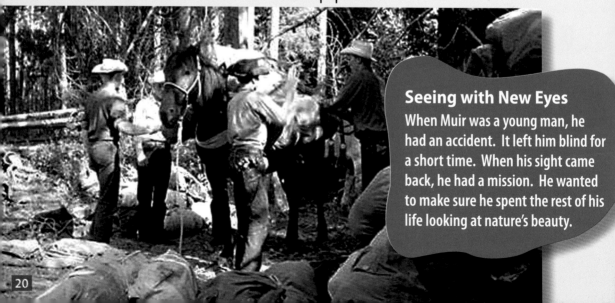

Seeing with New Eyes

When Muir was a young man, he had an accident. It left him blind for a short time. When his sight came back, he had a mission. He wanted to make sure he spent the rest of his life looking at nature's beauty.

Go Climb a Rock!

Millions of people visit Yosemite National Park each year. Thousands come to climb the huge rocks. Would you do it? Rock climbing takes great physical and mental strength. Imagine climbing straight up a 300 meter (984 foot) rock. It's like an interactive puzzle. The climber is looking for any crack in the rock to place his or her hand or foot. It requires a careful balance of skill and strength.

How do you learn to do this dangerous sport? The first step is to find an excellent teacher. Then read as much as you can on the topic. Watch other climbers. Ask them questions. Most importantly, take it slow. In this sport, it's better to be safe than sorry!

Greenpeace activists protesting offshore drilling in the Arctic Ocean

Today, the Sierra Club has almost a million members. The members work hard to protect our whole planet. There are many other groups that try to protect our planet, too. They include such groups as Greenpeace and the World Wildlife Federation. They teach about what is happening around the world. They share ideas about protecting our rainforests, oceans, and other wild land. These groups believe that humans must work together to protect Earth now and for the future.

Who Started It?

Rachel Carson is considered the mother of the environmental movement.

Where Are All the Frogs Going?

When all the animals of one kind die, it is called **extinction**. This has happened to many species. Sometimes natural processes make it happen. Other times humans do damage that endangers a species. For example, dinosaurs are extinct because of natural events. But scientists are now very worried about frogs. Nobody knows exactly why some are dying so fast. Pollution and global warming may be causes. Luckily, those are both things that people can change to save the frogs.

Julia "Butterfly" Hill

Julia Hill was born in 1974. She was in a car accident when she was 22. She almost died! After the accident, she felt she had a mission.

Hill decided to travel. She wanted to learn more about herself and the world. She went to the West Coast of the United States. She saw people trying to protect the redwood forest. The forest used to stretch more than 600 kilometers (400 miles). People were trying to cut it down. Hill joined the fight. She climbed one of the trees and named it Luna. She stayed in Luna for 738 days! Before her, no one stayed in a tree for more than 42 days.

At first, loggers were angry with her. In the end, they were friends. They made a deal to preserve some of the forest. She was able to preserve the forest, and she wasn't violent. Later, Hill started the Circle of Life Foundation. She wants people to work together to solve problems in the environment. Like Rachel Carson, she believes that all life is connected.

What Can You Do?

We can all do our part to keep Earth healthy. You can start by following the 3 Rs: **reduce**, **reuse**, and **recycle**.

Recycling is easy. It's one way to be sure you make less waste. Make an extra effort to put things in the recycle bin. You can put soda cans and water bottles there. Reduce the amount of trash you make. Try to buy things that will last for a long time and can be used again. Reuse everything you can. Binders and paper clips can be used again and again. Or you can donate things. Someone else might be able to use them. When you are finished with your books, pass them on to someone else. This is even better than recycling. It doesn't have to be remade before it can be used again.

If everyone makes a few small changes in how he or she cares for Earth, Earth will be stronger and healthier. Together, we can continue the work that Rachel Carson started.

A Wall of Trash

Americans throw away enough office paper each year to build a wall 3.5 meters (12 feet) high, going from Los Angeles to New York City. That's nearly 4,000 kilometers (2,459 miles).

⬆ Shredded paper is put in bales and processed at a recycling center.

Marjorie Stoneman Douglas

Marjorie Douglas was born in 1890. She was a writer who often wrote about environmental issues. She dedicated her life to preserving the Florida Everglades. At one time, people thought of the Everglades as useless swamp. People were going to drain the swamps so they could develop the land. Now, it's a national park.

Douglas started the Friends of the Everglades. It continues to fight to preserve the Everglades. Anyone can join the group for a small fee. The money helps to support the volunteers. Douglas died in 1998, but her work continues.

Marine Biologist: Sylvia Earle

Deep Ocean Engineering

Friends Down Deep

Sylvia Earle has swum with singing whales. She has also walked on the sea floor deeper than any other human! Earle has spent her whole career exploring our seas. What is her career? She's a scientist and explorer, and much more.

Earle is also an environmentalist. She wants to protect all living things that call the oceans home. Earle is an author and educator, too. And she's a businesswoman who started a submarine company. Earle has even given advice to presidents about how to care for our oceans.

▼ Earle shows a specimen to another scientist inside a research submarine.

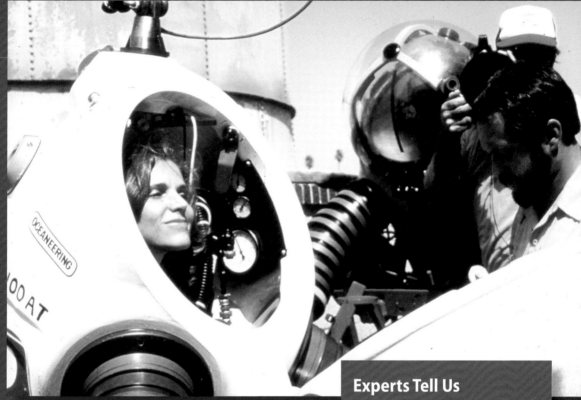

↑ Earle prepares for a deep dive in a special "JIM suit."

What does Earle want to be known as? "All of the above. *And* as somebody who cares."

Earle cares so much that she stopped eating seafood. "I know too many fish personally," she laughs.

Experts Tell Us

Earle says, "What really captured my attention as a kid is the enormous variety of life in the ocean."

Think About It

As a girl, Earle loved playing with horseshoe crabs on the beach even though they look scary. She says scientists need to be curious. Would you be a good scientist?

Did U Know?

The ocean contains 99% of all living species on the earth.

Lab: Acid Rain

This lab will explore the effects of acid rainfall on buildings and statues.

Materials

- clear glass
- six pieces of chalk (not the dustless type)
- water
- small bowl
- vinegar
- notebook and pencil
- clear, carbonated drink (lemon-lime soda or sparkling water)
- lemon juice

Procedure

1 Put one piece of chalk in the glass and add water so that the chalk is completely covered.

2 Put a second piece of chalk in the bowl and add enough vinegar so that the chalk is completely covered.

3 Observe the chalks for a few minutes for any changes. Then leave overnight.

4   On day two, record what you see. Do you see gas bubbles in the glass of chalk and water? Are there gas bubbles in the bowl with the vinegar? Where are the bubbles coming from?

5   Repeat the lab with a clear, carbonated drink. Is the carbon dioxide in the soda enough to break down the chalk?

6   Pour lemon juice over one piece of chalk and vinegar over another until the chalk breaks down. What is more acidic—lemon juice or vinegar?

Conclusion

Many old buildings and statues are made from marble, limestone, and sandstone. These materials have large amounts of calcium carbonate, which is also found in some brands of chalk. The acid in the rain can wash off part of the surface of buildings made with these materials. It can also cause corrosion on things made of metal such as cars and bridges. All rainwater is a little bit acidic. However, when rain is very acidic from the effects of pollution, it can do damage.

Glossary

accomplishment—something completed successfully

biology—the science of life and of living organisms and how they function and grow

chemical pesticides—a chemical used to kill pests, especially insects

civil service—a public servant; part of the field of public administration

DDT—a pesticide used widely in the United States in the 1940s and 1950s and banned after growing public concern over its environmental effects

deforestation—to cut down trees or forests on a large scale, faster than they can be replaced

ecosystem—all the living things in an area and how they interact with their environment

environment—the conditions that affect and influence the growth, development, and survival of organisms

extinction—the state in which a species no longer exists

food web—all of the different feeding relationships in an area

master's degree—a university degree that is higher than a bachelor's, usually needs at least two more years of school

natural resources—a material source of wealth, such as wood, fresh water, or oil, that has economic value

preservationist—one who advocates preservation, especially of natural areas, historical sites, or endangered species

recycle—sort and reprocess old material into new usable materials

reduce—the idea of choosing products that use less packaging

resistant—to not be affected by something

reuse—find a new use for a product without putting it in the trash or recycling it

Index

Sally Ride Science

Sally Ride Science™ is an innovative content company dedicated to fueling young people's interests in science. Our publications and programs provide opportunities for students and teachers to explore the captivating world of science—from astrobiology to zoology. We bring science to life and show young people that science is creative, collaborative, fascinating, and fun.

Image Credits